B. C. Lease

Between the Acts

A Comedy in Three Acts

B. C. Lease

Between the Acts
A Comedy in Three Acts

ISBN/EAN: 9783337054991

Printed in Europe, USA, Canada, Australia, Japan

Cover: Foto ©Andreas Hilbeck / pixelio.de

More available books at **www.hansebooks.com**

A Comedy in Three Acts

BY

B. C. LEASE

Phil

The Penn Pub

ARGUMENT.

"Dick" Comfort lives comfortably upon an allowance given him by his Uncle Meander, upon the condition that he shall not marry. Despite his uncle's wishes, he has fallen in love and married, being careful to keep the news from his uncle's ears.

He and his wife, Edith, have settled a few miles out of New York, and finding the time to hang heavy upon his hands, he occupies himself by writing a play, hoping thereby to win a prize that has been offered. This play he has completed, and all that is necessary is to revise it, which must be done by the evening of the day in which the story takes place. He has revised the first act and is taking a rest "Between the Acts," when the morning mail brings him a letter from his Uncle Meander, stating that he expects to arrive that very day to remain until the afternoon.

What is to be done? How is he to keep his uncle from seeing Edith, and so discover that they are married?

He finally decides that the only thing for him to do is to play bachelor.

He dispatches his wife to town upon an errand, having great difficulty in preventing his uncle from seeing her, who arrives just before she leaves. Shortly after George Merrigale, an old friend of Dick's, arrives, having run out from town to spend the day. He also is not aware that Dick is married. Seeing a picture of Edith he inquires who is the original, and Dick informs him that it is a photograph of the maid-servant. This deception is kept up throughout the play.

Later in the day Mrs. Meander, Dick's aunt, comes from town. She is not upon very friendly terms with her husband, and so took a later train. Edith also returns, and not knowing Dick's uncle and aunt, thinks Dick has sent her to town so that he could make love to another woman. The others take her for the maid, having been told so by Dick, and Merrigale misunderstanding a remark that Harris, the man-servant, has made, thinks Dick is not only married to his maid, but has another wife beside. He tells this to Meander, who is furious, and after an interview with Edith, dismisses his own wife, whom he does not recognize, and thinks is the other woman. Edith assists him in making peace with Mrs. Meander, and she is so sorry for mistrusting Dick that she willingly forgives him. Meander also, although blaming Dick, who is heartily sorry for the way he has acted, forgives him for Edith's sake, whom he pronounces "a jewel."

He tells Dick to continue writing plays for an amusement if he will, but when he is in need of the wherewithal to sustain life to draw upon him "Between the Acts."

3

TIME IN REPRESENTATION.
Two hours and a quarter.

COSTUMES.

"Dick" Comfort.—Ordinary suit.

George Merrigale.—1st, Traveling suit, spattered with mud ; 2d, Masquerading costume.

Alexander Meander.—Old gentleman's walking suit.

Harris.—Man servant suit.

Mrs. Clementina Meander.—Old fashioned dress, black bonnet, shawl, etc.

Mrs. Edith Comfort.—1st, House dress ; 2d, same with bonnet, etc.

Sally.—Servant's dress.

PROPERTIES.

Act I.—Letter for Comfort, which he is discovered reading ; a quantity of paper, writing materials, and cabinet photograph on table ; newspaper for Meander ; cigar for Merrigale to smoke ; boxes for Harris to enter with.

Act II.—Dusting-brush for Harris ; money for Comfort to give Harris ; handkerchief for Merrigale ; bag for Sally.

Act III.—Newspaper for Merrigale ; glass of water on table for Comfort.

4

CAST OF CHARACTERS.

"DICK" COMFORT, *married, yet single.*

GEORGE MERRIGALE, *an unfriendly friend.*

ALEXANDER MEANDER, *Dick's uncle. Blamed but blameless.*

HARRIS, *Comfort's man-servant.*

MRS. CLEMENTINA MEANDER, *Dick's aunt. Blameless, but blamed.*

EDITH COMFORT, *Dick's wife. "Unknown, unhonored, and unsung."*

SALLY, *Mrs. Meander's Maid.*

ACT I AND II—MORNING. ACT III—AFTERNOON.

STAGE DIRECTIONS.

R.	R. C.	C.	L. C.	L.

The player is supposed to face the audience. R., means right; L., left; C., centre; R. C., right of centre; L. C., left of centre; D. F., door in flat or scene across back of stage; R. D., right door; L. D., left door; L. D. 1, left door, 1st entrance; L. D. 2, left door, 2d entrance.

5

BETWEEN THE ACTS.

ACT I.

SCENE.—*Handsomely furnished drawing-room in* DICK COMFORT'S *house.* COMFORT *discovered standing by table, reading letter attentively.*

COMFORT (*after pause*) What shall I do? Here is a letter from Uncle Meander, stating that he is coming to spend the day. When he told me, four years ago, that I should be his heir and that he would allow me $2,500 a year during his lifetime, I raised no objection whatever; in fact the idea rather pleased me. But there was to be one condition—that I should never marry. I had no desire to marry then; that was four years ago. But one can't help falling in love; (*pointing to himself*) at least *this one* couldn't. Who wouldn't fall in love with Edith? And ever since Edith and I were married, six months ago, I have been in constant fear and trembling lest Uncle should hear of it. This visit will upset all my calculations. He will discover the truth and then my chances of succession will vanish. What is to be done? (*Reads letter*) "Will arrive Thursday morning"—that is to-day—"and will be compelled to leave by the afternoon train." The afternoon train goes at four o'clock. (*Thoughtfully*) Now, if I could prevent a meeting between Edith and Uncle Meander; if I could play the part of a bachelor, just for to-day—by George! I have half a mind to try it; that is my only chance; my last hope. I'll do it. But what is to be done with Edith? (*Enter* MRS. COMFORT, D. L. 2.)

MRS. C. Dick (COM. *starts*), won't you take a drive with me this morning?

COM. My dear Edith, I—I fear I am too busy this morning.

MRS. C. You do not appear so.

COM. Well, in this case, appearances are deceitful. I—I

7

am devoting myself to-day to the revising of my comedy. It has to be sent in to-morrow, you know; that's why I am working so hard. I have just finished making the necessary corrections in Act I, so I thought I was entitled to a few minutes rest.

MRS. C. Oh! I wish you had never begun to write your old play. Suppose you should win the prize, what good would it do you?

COM. But, my dear Edith, think of the fame.

MRS. C. And of what use would that be to you? Would it help you remember your wife? Would you think of her happiness any more than you do now?

COM. No, not more than now, for you know that to see my wife happy is my greatest wish. I would enjoy a drive in your company, far more than working all day, but duty before pleasure, you know, work before play.

MRS. C. But your play is before everything.

COM. And yet, it is not recreation. My play is work—very hard work, too; but, on the other hand, my work is all play, so it is the combination of these two evils that makes me, in your eyes, a dull boy. But I—I am very glad that you intend to take a drive. It is such beautiful weather; suppose you drive into town and spend the day with your mother.

MRS. C. Why, I wouldn't get home until late this afternoon.

COM. (*half aside*) Yes, I know.

MRS. C. Besides, I spent all last week in town. No, unless you will go with me, I shall not take a drive to-day.

COM. But, my dear Edith, there is a little commission I want you to execute for me in town. I—I need some paper, in fact, I must have it, or I can't finish my play to-night.

MRS. C. You have plenty of paper; look here. (*Takes up a quantity of paper from table.*)

COM. (*confused*) Yes—but—a—but this is not the right kind.

MRS. C. What kind do you wish?

COM. Oh! any kind will do; buy all kinds.

MRS. C. But Dick, can't Harris purchase it, just as well as I?

COM. No, no, you are the only one that can do it, that is to say, you are the one I wish to go to town, I—I—mean—oh! (*earnestly*) Edith, if you love me, do go.

MRS. C. Very well, my dear, if you wish it; but I shall

take the train, it is too long a drive. How much paper shall I buy?

Com. Oh! any amount; I shall need a great quantity; as much as you can bring home. (*Aside*) The more she purchases the longer it will take her.

Mrs. C. (*aside*) Poor boy, he is so nervous; he has been working entirely too hard.

Com. (*looking at watch*) Nine o'clock! You will just have time to catch the train. I shall order the carriage to take you to the depot. (*Calling*) Harris!

Mrs. C. But, Dick, the train doesn't leave until nine thirty.

Com. Yes—you can just make it, no more. (*Calling*) Harris!

Mrs. C. There is plenty of time. (*Exit* Mrs. C. D. L. 1.)

Com. (*calling loudly*) Harris! (*Enter* Harris D. F.)

Har. Did you ring, sir?

Com. (*sharply*) No, I didn't ring, but I have been calling you for the last half-hour.

Har. Yes, sir.

Com. Order the carriage immediately.

Har. Yes, sir. (*Aside*) His honor is in good spirits this mornin'. (*Exit* Harris, D. F.)

Com. If Edith will only leave before Uncle Meander arrives all will be well (*takes up MS. from table*) Here's my comedy; two acts yet to revise before to-night. Oh! why did uncle choose to-day for a visit! I will be too busy to entertain him, he must amuse himself. I suppose I had better work while I have the opportunity (*sits at table*) Let me see, Act I is completed; I am glad of it. Now for Act II (*takes up pen, stops as if listening*) Carriage-wheels! Can it be Uncle Meander (*rises and goes to window in back of stage*)! By George! it must be he; that is the hack from the depot. Now what am I to do?

Mrs. C. (*calling from without*) Dick!

Com. (*coming down stage*) Yes, my dear; no hurry; there is plenty of time. (*Aside*) I must resort to desperate measures (*locks door* L. 1). There, she is caged. (*Enter* Meander D. F.)

Mean. Well, Richard, my boy, here I am.

Com. Ah! uncle! I am delighted. You're looking as hale and hearty as ever, I see.

Mean. Yes, never was in better health. You needn't hope to get rid of me for many years, although, no doubt, you wish it, you young rascal (*digs him in the ribs*).

Com. (*deprecatingly*) O uncle!

MEAN. Well, Richard, it has been four years since last I saw you. You're not married yet I hope.

COM. (*nervously*) Married! The idea of my marrying. Oh! no I—

MRS. C. (*calling from without*) Dick!

COM. (*coughs violently*).

MEAN. Did any one call?

COM. (*confused*) No, oh! no! that's only the parrot. (*Aside*) How shall I prevent them from meeting? (*To* MEANDER) Uncle, you must be very tired after your journey (*taking him by the arm*): I am sure you would like to rest awhile (*leading him toward* D. R.) Come; right in here.

MEAN. (*hesitatingly*) But, my dear boy, I really do not feel fatigued.

COM. Oh! yes; I am sure you do.

MRS. C. (*calling from without*) Dick!

COM. (*nervously*) The parrot, only the parrot; speaks very plainly, doesn't it?

MEAN. Do you keep it in a cage?

COM. Yes, oh! yes; she is caged! I—I mean *it* is. Right in here, uncle (*pushes him into room* R., *shuts door and locks it*). Now *he's* caged. What shall I do with them? I will dispose of Edith first (*goes to* D. L. I *and unlocks it carefully*). Edith, my dear, you must make haste. (*Calls*) Harris! (*Enter* MRS. C. D. L. I. *Dressed ready to go out.*)

COM. You will lose the train. (*Enter* HARRIS, D. F.)

MRS. C. But, Dick, you said there was plenty of time.

COM. So there *was*, but—a—there is no time now. (*To* HARRIS) Harris, is the carriage ready

HARRIS. It is at the door, sir.

COM. (*sharply*) That's what I asked you. (*To* MRS. C.) Good-bye, my dear (*kisses her*). You won't return until this evening, will you? No, that's right; I won't expect you until then. (MEAN. *pounds upon door.*)

MRS. C. What's that?

COM. (*confused*) Oh! that's—a—that's only the dog.

HARRIS. No, sir; I just seen the dog down—

COM. Keep quiet! do you hear! I've had enough of your impudence this morning. (*To* MRS. C.) Good-bye, Edith (*kisses her again*). Spend the day at your mother's. Good-bye (*hurries her out* D. F.; *exit* HARRIS D. F.)

MEAN. (*pounds on the door and calls*) Richard!

COM. The dog is becoming noisy; Edith left just in time. (*Unlocks door* R.) Why, uncle, what is the matter? (*Enter* MEAN. D. R.) Did you lock yourself in?

MEAN. (*with suppressed temper*) Lock myself in! No, certainly not! how could I, when the key was on the outside?

COM. (*holding key in hand*) So it is. It was a mistake. Harris must have done it; what a stupid fellow he is! I have given instructions that these doors be always kept closed, and Harris, with his natural craving to obey orders, must have locked you in.

MEAN. Well, your servant's yearning to be obedient was misdirected in this case; see that it does not occur again.

COM. (*half aside*) I hope there will be no necessity.

MEAN. There was no necessity *this* time.

COM. (*quickly*) No, of course not, of course not.

MEAN. (*suspiciously*) By the way, Richard, I heard a woman's voice; whose was it?

COM. That was the parrot.

MEAN. But the parrot is not in this room. This was a woman—I am sure of it; she was talking to some man.

COM. (*confusca*) Oh! it—I mean she was—Harris, you know—the maid talking to Harris. (*Earnestly*) But, uncle, you couldnt't understand what they said, could you?

MEAN. No, not perfectly. I thought I heard the man say "good-bye."

COM. That was to the maid, you know, she was going to spend the day in town.

MEAN. Then the man spoke of a dog; do you keep dogs?

COM. Oh! yes, about a dozen.

MEAN. A dozen dogs and a parrot! You seem to be fond of the animal kingdom. Any others?

COM. Not that I can think of at present. You see, I—I live such a quiet and retired life I find it necessary to have some companions.

MEAN. You evidently believe in quantity before quality. I am glad that your companions are chosen from among the brute creation, from the animals that are blessed with being created dumb; there is a kind of animal—about which I have often warned you—whose oratorical powers are very great. In that animal's eyes we *men* are considered as members of the brute creation.

COM. (*deprecatingly*) O uncle! how very ungallant.

MEAN. It's true nevertheless; take your servant for example—(*enter* HARRIS, D. F.)—with all his dumbness he is far superior to—

HAR. Mr. Comfort, sir!

COM. (*turning*) What do you mean, you rascal!

Har.   There's a gent—

Com.   Silence!

Har.   Yes, sir, but—

Com.   Did you hear me?

Har.   Yes, sir, but Mr. Marygal told me to—

Com.   Merrigale! George Merrigale!

Har.   I don' know, sir; but he just arriv'.

Com.   Why didn't you say so?

Har.   I was attemptin' to, sir, but—

Com.   You're too confounded slow.

Har.   Yes, sir.

Com.   Show Mr. Merrigale up immediately—now don't ask me " when "—immediately! (*Exit* HARRIS, D. F.)

Com. (*To* MEAN.) George is an old friend of mine, uncle; I haven't seen him for a year. (*Aside suddenly recollecting*) Deuce take it all! He knows all about my marriage; he will ruin me. (*Aloud*) Uncle, you didn't half rest yourself did you? (*taking him by the arm*) Come, take another nap.

Mean.   But I feel no need of rest.

Com.   Then take a walk over the grounds; I know you will enjoy it; right out this way. (*Leads him toward* R.)

Mean.   No, Richard, I would far rather remain. (*Enter* MERRIGALE, D. F., *clothing spattered with mud.*)

Mer.   Ah! Dickie, my boy. I've come in the shape of a little surprise; it is a surprise, isn't it?

Com.   Yes, I must confess it is.

Mer.   I knew it. Haven't seen you for nearly a year, have I? How am I looking, eh?

Com.   A trifle seedy.

Mer.   Eh! I knew you would say so. You must excuse my good looks; (*pointing to mud*) these beauty marks were gathered along the road.

What a deuced slow place you have out here, old fellow; I had to walk all the way from the depot. Only one cab, and some old duffer took that, so I had to foot it (*seeing* MEAN, *aside*) By jove! there he is. (*To* COMFORT) Present us, old man.

Com. (*aside*) There is no escape. (*To* MEAN.) Uncle, let me introduce an old friend of mine, Mr. Merrigale.

Mer.   The honor is mine, sir. (*Aside*) Dick's uncle! A —Mr. Comfort, I suppose.

Mean. (*crossly*) I never claimed it.

Mer.   Quite right, sir.

Mean. (*with dignity*) I consider the title which you have just applied to me very inappropriate, sir.

MER. You mean, "old duffer"? Oh! don't let that make you uneasy; you couldn't help it, you know.

MEAN. (*aside*) A very forward fellow.

COM. (*anxious to get* MER. *out of the room*) George, I know you would like to change your clothes.

MER. Why, I've scarcely had time to shake hands with you yet, old fellow (*takes his hand*). I am stopping in ―――― for a few days, and thought I would just run out and see an old friend. Too slow out here for me, though. I'd petrify in a few days. Ah! Dickie! we don't have the lively times we used to, do we? What a gay bird you were!

COM. Perhaps I was before I—ahem—

MER. Married, eh!

COM. (*coughs violently*).

MER. Don't be bashful, old man (*looking around*). Where do you keep her? I never saw her, you know; left home just after the engagement was announced and went to India.

COM. (*coughs again*).

MER. Bad cough that, old man.

MEAN. Mr. Merriwind, may I ask to whose engagement you were referring?

COM. (*aside*) It is all over with me.

MER. Certainly, sir. To Dick's; sly dog, isn't he? Always was a gay sort of a chap, you know, but I never thought he cared for the ladies. The first I knew, he was engaged.

MEAN. Richard, you told me nothing of this (*sternly*). Have you deceived me, sir?

COM. O uncle! pray spare my feelings.

MEAN. (*aside*) He appears agitated. (*Aloud*) Was the engagement broken off? Did it end as most of these love affairs do?

COM. Yes, sir—it—a—it came to a sudden end—about six months ago. (*Aside*) I was married then. (*To* MERRIGALE) George, won't you please go and change your clothing?

MER. Certainly, old chap, but—a—this is the only suit I have with me.

COM. I will lend you one. (*Calling*) Harris!

MER. Awful sorry for my mistake, old man.

COM. A very natural one, but—a—please make no more. (*Enter* HARRIS D. F.) (*To* HARRIS) Harris show Mr. Merrigale to my room. George, I think I left one of my suits on a chair; you can wear that while yours is being cleaned.

HAR. Yes, sir. (*Exeunt* HARRIS *and* MERRIGALE D. L. 2.)

MEAN. Now, Richard, explain matters! Why did you not notify me of your engagement?

COM. (*confused*) Well, uncle, I—I—I can hardly tell; you were away at the time, you know.

MEAN. Did *you* end the engagement or the girl?

COM. It was by mutual consent; I—I think perhaps I was the more anxious of the two.

MEAN. I am very glad that it *did* end. You know that a wife would only make trouble between us.

COM. Yes, I know.

MEAN. Never let me hear of your marriage, or—you know the consequences.

COM. I am doing my best and I assure you, uncle, that ever since my—a—my—engagement came to an end I have never once thought of another woman.

MEAN. That's right, Richard; you show your good sense. What time does the next train arrive from town?

COM. (*looking at watch*) There was one due a few minutes ago.

MEAN. That is the one my wife was to take.

COM. (*surprised*) Your wife! Not Aunt Clementina!

MEAN. Of course; how many wives do you credit me with?

COM. But you said nothing about her coming. '

MEAN. Didn't I mention it in my letter? That was a great oversight. She stopped in town; said she would come in the next train.

COM. (*aside*) I seem to be holding a reception to-day.

MEAN. In case, Richard, you notice anything peculiar in my actions toward my wife, do not be alarmed; we have had a little misunderstanding and at present do not speak.

COM. That's too bad.

MEAN. Oh! no; it's a little pleasantry on her part, that's all. You may perhaps think it affectation, but through force of habit it has become a second nature. And, by the way, should she inquire if you " know who that individual is "— which means me—it would be just as well for you to plead ignorance.

COM. What do you mean? You want me to act as if you were a stranger?

MEAN. Oh! no, that will be unnecessary. Just tell her —if she should ask the question—that you do not know me. She will like you all the better for it and it won't hurt my feelings in the slightest; that is another second nature.

But if you do not object, we will drop the subject of wives, Richard.

Com. Willingly, sir.

Mean. That parrot of yours—is it a Chrysotis or an Erithacus?

Com. (*bewildered*) Just a—a plain green one, sir; a talking one, you know.

Mean. I should like very much to see it. (*Enter* Harris D. L. 2.)

Com. (*confused*) I—I am very sorry, but—

Mean. No butting, Richard, your man can bring it. (To Harris) James, bring the parrot.

Har. (*surprised*) The which, sir?

Mean. The parrot.

Har. I—I am afraid, sir—

Com. (*quickly*) Afraid! of what? bring the bird instantly.

Har. You mean the stuffed one in the library, sir?

Com. Stuff and nonsense! the one in the—a—the right wing.

Har. (*bewildered*) Ye-es, sir.

Com. Be quick now, and don't return without it.

Har. Yes, sir. (*Exit* D. F.)

Mean. Have you more than one parrot?

Com. Oh! yes, half a dozen; I—I quite overlooked the others. (*Enter* Mer. D. L. 2, *dressed in clown's costume.*)

Mer. Is this the best you could do for me, old man?

Com. Why what in the deuce have you got on?

Mer. That is more than I can tell you. This is the suit I found on the chair. Your man took my suit before I had a chance to look for yours; then it was this or nothing. I preferred this.

Com. I am glad you gave it the preference. But I didn't mean that suit. That is a masquerading costume. (*Beginning to laugh*) George you look like a perfect clown.

Mer. And so I am—I—I—mean—say Dickie, it is hardly kind to dress me up just for your own amusement.

Com. (*still laughing*) Forgive me, old fellow, but do take off those ridiculous garments.

Mer. Oh! I quite enjoy them; makes me feel young again, you know (*dances to table, sees photograph of* Mrs. C. *and examines it*).

Mean. (*To* Com.) He *acts* young; childish, I should call it.

Mer. I say, Dickie, who is she? Deuced fine looking girl.

Com. (*aside*) My wife's photograph! (*coughs violently then quickly*) As I was saying, uncle, I am exceedingly fond of parrots, in fact, I make them a specialty. The green ones are my favorites, I think; they are so—a—so green, you know.

Mer. (*coming down stage with photograph in hand*) Who did you say she was, Dickie? Any relation?

Com. (*feigning ignorance*) Relation! Who! What!

Mer. Why this stunning looking girl (*showing photograph to* Mean. *and digging him in ribs*) A beauty, eh!

Com. (*looking at photograph*) Where did you find that?

Mer. On the table; who is she?

Com. (*at a loss what to say*) She—it, I mean—no—that is to say she is—a—the maid-servant, only the maid-servant.

Mer. Maid-servant! By jove, she is far too good looking for a maid-servant (*handing photograph to* Mean.) What do you think of that, eh? (*digs him in ribs*) looks like a princess in disguise, don't she?

Mean. But, Richard, how comes a picture of a maid-servant on your sitting-room table? I do not admire your taste.

Com. I really don't know; I—I suppose Harris must have left it there. No doubt she gave it to him and he forgot it.

Mean. A very careless fellow.

Com. Yes, very.

Mer. (*gazing at photograph*) What's the fair creature's name, Dickie?

Com. (*hesitating*) A—a—Sallie.

Mer. Pretty name; can't we see her, old man? Come, now, trot her out.

Com. Impossible!

Mer. Oh! do now.

Com. Impossible, I tell you. She has gone to town. (*Aside*) I have told more lies to-day than is good for my health.

Mer. When will she return?

Com. (*sharply*) It appears to me, Merrigale, you take a great interest in my—my maid.

Mer. I do.

Com. (*aside*) I am becoming positively afraid of that man's questions. A few more and he will discover—

Mer. I say, Dickie, can't you tell me—

Com. (*interrupting*) No, I can't. I—I am very sorry, but —a—not now, there is something that requires my attention. (*Aside*) That's another lie; I am getting in over my head; it will be best for me to withdraw from this man's cross-questioning, until he changes the subject. (*Aloud*) Gentlemen, I hope you will excuse me for a moment; I shall return presently. (*Exit* D. L. 2.)

MER. It's a shame that such a clipper of a girl should spend her days as a maid-servant, don't you think so?

MEAN. (*sharply*) I don't think anything about it. (*Takes newspaper from pocket, sits and reads.*)

MER. I knew you would say so; of course you don't *think* anything about it; neither do I, we *know* it. How would *you* like to live in solitude as a maid-servant, eh? (*Waits for reply*) Just imagine yourself a maid-servant; you wouldn't like it, would you? Of course, I mean, if you were accustomed to better things (*confused*), that is to say, I—I—mean—(*looks at* MEAN., *who pays no attention*) (*aside*) I hardly think it is worth my while to mean anything; he doesn't appear to be interested. (*A pause*) (*sitting*). This is rather slow. (*Enter* HARRIS D. F., *closely followed by* MRS. MEAN. *and* SALLIE.)

HAR. Mrs. Clementina Meander, sir! (MEAN. *starts, but continues to read paper.* MER. *rises.*)

MRS. MEAN. (*screams*) Sarah, what is that creature!

SAL. One of thim ring circus clowns, mum.

HAR. If that ain't Mr. Marygal, disguised. (*To* MER.) I won't tell her who you are, sir.

MER. Disguised! Nonsense! I am Mr. George Merrigale, madam, at your service.

MRS. M. (*patronizingly*) I think you can hardly be of any service to me, my man.

HAR. This is Mr. Comfort's friend, Mr. Marygal, mam. (*To* MER.) I thought you were disguised, sir.

MRS. M. Mr. Comfort's friend!

HAR. That's what I remarked, mam.

MRS. M. Sarah, did he say Mr. Comfort's friend?

SAL. Indade, thet's jist what he did said, mum.

MRS. M. (*half aside*) What must his enemies be like! (*Exit* HAR. D. F. *laughing.*)

MER. Madam, I am exceedingly sorry that I should have caused you and your daughter any annoyance.

MRS. M. My daughter! This is my French maid. (SAL. *curtesies*, MEAN. *begins to whistle.*)

MRS. M. (*starts*) Sarah, who is that individual?

SAL. Sure an' I don't know, mum; sounds like some whistlin' stame dummy. (MEAN. *appears insulted and stops whistling.*)

MER. That's Mr. Comfort, Dick's uncle, you know.

2

MRS. M.   Comfort!   Sarah, did he say Comfort?

SAL.   Indade he did, mum.

MRS. M.   A blackbird may think it is disguised by calling itself an eagle, but I am not to be deceived; I know
a blackbird when I see one.   (*To* MEAN.) Do you hear
me?

MER.   Oh! yes, I—I hear! of course you do.   (*Aside*)
What is she talking about?

SAL.   And I know a blackbird, too, mum.

MER.   Certainly; so do I.   (*Aside*) There is nothing so
very remarkable about that.   (*To* MRS. MEAN.) I will present the gentleman, madam.   (MEAN. *appears uncomfort-
able.*)

MRS. M.   Stop! young man, you know not what you are
about to do.

MER.   Oh! yes'm, I do!

MRS. M.   That—that person and I are strangers.

MER.   Yes, I know, but—

MRS. M.   And I prefer that we should remain strangers.
(*To* MEAN.) Do you hear me, sir?   Strangers forever!

MER.   I—I beg your pardon.   I—I do not wish to force
his acquaintance upon you.   I think, however, you would
find him a pleasant companion, but, of course, just as you
please.   (*Aside*) Seems a little eccentric.

MRS. M.   Sarah, he knows my wishes upon the subject,
does he not?

SAL.   Iny common, horse-sensed individual would,
mum.   (MEAN. *starts whistling.*)

MRS. M.   That—that creature is making those peculiar
noises again; they give me the shivers.

MER. (*To* MEAN.) My dear sir, won't you postpone your
music until a more auspicious moment?   This lady
seriously objects.   (MEAN. *continues to whistle.   Enter
COMFORT D. L. 2.*)

COM.   Ah! my dear aunt!

MER. (*aside*)   Dick's aunt!

COM.   I have not kept you waiting long, I hope.

MRS. M. (*embracing him*)   A very long time, Richard; a
very long time.

COM.   But I feel confident that my friend Merrigale has
entertained you.

MRS. M.   Your friend!   Is he indeed your friend!   (*To*
SAL.) Sarah, have my ears deceived me?   I understood
him to call this—this person his friend.

SAL.   Yez eared aright, mum, " me frind " is jist what he
was sayin'.

Mrs. M. O Richard! how low you have fallen. Alas! how true it is, "a man is known by the company he keeps." I little thought your friends would be found among circus clowns and—a—horse jockeys. (MEAN. *controls laughter with difficulty.*)

. MER. But, my dear madam—

COM. Why, aunt, you do not understand. Mr. Merrigale is neither a horse jockey nor a clown, but a gentleman of leisure. His clothes were so dirty that I insisted upon his wearing one of my suits, but by mistake he put on a masquerading costume. Looks funny, doesn't he? (*Laughs and is joined by* MEAN.)

MEAN. (*aside*) The idea! took him for a circus clown! Served him right though.

Mrs. M. (*with dignity*) It seems strange that a gentleman of means, such as you hold your friend to be, should wear unclean clothing, and I cannot imagine why you should have in your possession such a costume. (MEANDER *laughs.*) Richard, who is that individual?

COM. That! why you know, that's—(*suddenly recollecting*), I—I—I really don't know, aunt.

MEAN. (*aside*) He just saved himself.

MER. (*aside*) What's Dickie talking about?

Mrs. M. I am pleased that you do not know him; he has done nothing but insult me ever since I entered the house.

COM. Insult you!

SAL. Thet's jist what I belave he has bin a-doin', as we all on us knows.

Mrs. M. He is very objectionable, Richard; please see that he is removed. (MEAN. *whistles.*)

COM. (*haughtily*) Would you be so kind as to absent yourself, sir. (*Aside to* MEAN.) Uncle, you'll find some choice cigars in the smoking-room.

MEAN. (*rising*) I never smoke, but I shall withdraw from this apartment with great pleasure. (*Exit* D. R.)

COM. George, I know that you are partial to a good cigar—

MER. Yes, your knowledge is correct; you know my weakness, and if you will excuse me, I will join your uncle. (*Exit* D. R.)

Mrs. M. (*throwing her arms around* COMFORT) O Richard! my life is not a happy one!

SAL. Nor moine, nather. mum.

Mrs. M. Sarah, you will refrain from those unnecessary remarks.

SAL. I—I was mainen on account of 'im, mum; and sayin' yez a-pinin' yez own swate silf away, mum.

MRS. M. Yes, alas! it is too true! Here, Sarah, take my hat and shawl (*gives them to her. Beginning to cry*) I am pining myself into a shadow; I am so ill-treated.

COM. That's too bad. Do you have many—many quarrels?

MRS. M. (*crying*) Their name is legion.

SAL. For they are many. She quarrels with 'im all the toime, sor.

MRS. M. (*sternly*) Sarah! *I* never quarrel.

SAL. In course yez don't, mum; it's 'im thet quarrels.

MRS. M. (*throwing her arms around* COM. *and laying her head on his shoulder*) I am so ill-treated that I have not where to lay my weary head.

COM. (*aside*) She appears to have had practice somewhere.

MRS. M. Even my husband considers me a burden.

COM. (*aside*) She is a trifle heavy.

MRS. M. I have become in his eyes his servant; a mere dependent.

COM. (*aside*) She acts like a hanger-on.

MRS. M. Ah, Richard, if you were married, you would understand.

COM. (*starting*) Married! ha-ha, the idea of my marrying. (*Enter* MRS. C. D. F.)

MRS. M. But you will marry some day. (*Enter* MEAN. *and* MER. D. R., MER. *smoking.*)

COM. But I am *not* married, nor have I any desire to be. (MRS. C. *screams.*)

MRS. M. (*turning*) Richard, who is this woman?

COM. (*confused*) Oh! that—a—she—you know—she is my—my *maid-servant.* (*Enter* HAR. D. F. *carrying boxes.* MRS. C. *leans against him.*) *Tableau.*

Act II.

SCENE.—*Same as Act I. Boxes piled by table.* HARRIS *discovered dusting.*

HAR. I can't understand it. The governor never acted like this before; leastwise not since I've knowed him. He must have somethin' on his mind—that is, on part of his mind—I'm afear'd the t'other part h'aint there. (*Tapping his forehead*) I'm afeared he's just a little queer kinder, as it were. The idea of blamin' everything on me, when I never done nothin'; and then talking about parrots and one thing an' another; tellin' me go fetch the parrot in the right wing an' not to come back until I done it. Dog me cats! I'd never have got back at all if it hadn't a-been for the missus, an' them boxes. (*Looking at boxes by table*) Just look at 'em; I had to carry 'em up-stairs two at onct, and it warn't no easy job, nuther. Wonder what's in 'em? (*Examines.*) (*Enter* COM. D. L. 2.)

COM. (*sharply*) Harris! (HAR. *starts*) Leave those boxes alone!

HAR. Yes, sir; I was goin' to—when you came in—

COM. You were going to do nothing of the kind. (*Goes to table.*)

HAR. Goin' to do what, sir?

COM. (*angrily*) Leave the room!

HAR. No, sir; I warn't.

COM. Leave the room, do you hear!

HAR. (*meekly*) Yes, sir (*aside*) I'm afeared he's a little touched in the 'ead, as it were (*going*).

COM. (*calling*) Harris!

HAR. (*stopping*) Yes, sir.

COM. (*sitting*) You may think that I have been acting in —a—a somewhat peculiar manner to-day.

HAR. Seein' as it were you, sir, I didn't think nothin' on it.

COM. (*angrily*) What!

HAR. I—I mean, sir, it warn't for me to think. You can act as it pleases you, sir.

COM. Oh! I can?

HAR. Yes, sir.

COM. (*dryly*) Thank you.

21

HAR. (*surprised*) Sir!

COM. I said, "Thank you."

HAR. Yes, sir. (*Aside*) I'm sure I don't know what he's thankin' me for.

COM. Perhaps I may have blamed you for one or two little things that you did not do.

HAR. If I might be so bold, sir, I will say, that now you speak on it, perhaps there was one or two little matters that I didn't hexactly know what your meanin' were.

COM. (*thoughtfully*) Yes, perhaps there were, but— they were necessary.

HAR. Yes, sir. (*Hesitating*) A-a might I ask, sir, what parrot I was to fetch by the wing, as it were?

COM. Never mind the parrot, Harris; it is an unpleasant subject. (*Gives money*) Here, take this.

HAR. (*aside*) He is certainly crazy.

COM. And be sure and say nothing to the other servants of this conversation. Now you may leave the room.

HAR. Thank ye, sir. (*Exit* D. F.)

COM. What a dumb-head that fellow is. By George! here's my play; I had forgotten it. My rest, between the acts, has been a long one, but it can hardly be called a rest; never worked harder in my life. Since I started upon my diplomatic career—we will give it the benefit of the doubt and call it diplomacy—I have told so many lies that now they come without my assistance—in fact, they almost say themselves, and I have great difficulty in keeping them back. They are cheap, but very useful; the question is whether I won't have to pay for them some day. I am afraid the bill will be a large one, for I keep a running account. Now that Edith has returned, my ingenuity will be taxed to its utmost. How in the deuce did Edith get back so soon? She must have bought the paper in the village; I'll wager the stationer made his fortune. I have said nothing to her since her return; haven't had the chance, and I can't say that I desire one. (*Enter* MRS. C. D. L. I, *goes toward* D. F.) COM. (*rising*) By jove! the chance has come (*getting in her way*). My dear Edith, I—

MRS. C. (*very haughtily*) Sir!

COM. (*stepping aside quickly*) I—I merely wished to inquire if you—you had paid the freight on these boxes.

MRS. C. I have no reply to make. (*Exit* D. F.)

COM. Phew! I feel crushed (*sits at table*) (*trying to laugh*) Ha-ha-ha-; I don't care; it's a good joke (*laughing very weakly*) ha-ha (*picks up pen*) I must work (*starts to write.*) MER. *entering* D. R. *on tiptoe, still in clown's costume.*)

COM. (*throwing pen on floor*) Confound it! I have no ideas.

MER. Shew! That's nothing new. Don't make such a noise, old man; you'll waken him.

COM. Waken whom?

MER. Your uncle; I left him in the smoking-room, trying to raise the roof. My, how he does snore. I was telling him one of my best stories, too, and would you believe it, he fell fast asleep.

COM. That was only natural.

MER. Very unnatural I call it. The story was good; about a man, you know, that—

COM. (*interrupting*) Sorry, George, but I am very busy to-day, please postpone your interesting tale.

MER. Well, I want—

COM. No stories, George; (*aside*) I have a monopoly on stories.

MER. All right then, some other time; but I wan't to ask you about that maid-servant, I would like to—

COM. (*angrily*) Hang the maid-servant!

MER. Hang her! oh! no, I—

COM. Then shoot her!

MER. Why, Dick, old fellow, what ails you?

COM. Nothing. (*A pause*) If you really must know the truth about her I suppose I will have to tell you. (*Aside*) Now for another lie. (*To* MER.) She is a relation of mine.

MER. Oh! that accounts for your interest in her.

COM. My interest! It strikes me you show the more interest of the two.

MER. But how is it that she is in your employ as a servant?

COM. (*hesitating*) Well—she is not exactly my maid.

MER. Your housekeeper perhaps.

COM. (*quickly*) Yes, my housekeeper. (*Aside*) Why didn't I think of that before. (*To* MER.) She was poor and alone in the world, you know, so I thought it was only charitable to give her a home. I tell you this, Merrigale, so that in case you notice any familiarity on her part toward me you will understand.

MER. Yes, certainly. I knew she was not an ordinary servant; and, by the way, old man, I'm afraid you hurt her feelings by calling her a maid; these poor relations are often very sensitive, you know.

COM. It was rather unkind, I admit. (*Aside, looking off* D. F.) By jove! here she comes. I must keep them from meeting. (*To* MER.) George, quick, hide yourself! (*Taking his arm*) Here, back of this screen!

MER. What's the matter, old man?

COM. My—my housekeeper is coming.

MER. I don't mind meeting her.

COM. Yes, but I—I wish to apologize to her, and I would rather do it without your assistance. Make haste! (*Pushes* MER. *back of screen*) (*Enter* MRS. C. D. F.—COM. *leans against table and looks in another direction.*)

MRS. C. (*after pause, pleadingly*) Dick!

COM. Please don't call me Dick. You know I never like you to call me by my first name before company, I—I mean when we have company.

MRS. C. Why, Dick!

COM. There you go again.

MRS. C. You know I always call you "Mr. Comfort" before people, but (*looking around*)—but there's no one here.   ·

COM. (*quickly*) Of course there isn't. (*Nervously*) Who—who said there was?

MRS. C. Oh! won't you tell me what is the matter? What have I done? Are you ill?

COM. No, certainly not.

. MRS. C. Then why do you act so strangely? Why did you call me a maid?

COM. That was a mistake, a lapsus lingua—I—I am sorry.

MRS. C. Won't you kiss me and tell me you love me?

COM. (*coughs nervously*) Why, of course not; I—I couldn't do that.

MRS. C. (*beginning to cry*) Don't you love me, Dick?

COM. (*aside*) What will George think of this? (*To* MRS. C.) Now you mustn't act that way. We have talked this matter over before, and you know my feelings toward you perfectly well; it would not only be utterly useless for me to tell you that I loved you, but—a—but under the circumstances, ridiculous.

MRS. C. (*stopping crying*) I see it all; you do not love me. You sent me out of the house so that you could make love to another woman. Who was that woman? (*Becoming excited*) You are afraid to tell me.

COM. You ought to know who she is.

MRS. C. You have forgotten the woman you once loved. You have forgotten her whom you promised to—

COM. I promised nothing; you are talking nonsense.

MRS. C. Oh! of course, you say so.

Com. I am perfectly willing to tell you who the lady was.

Mrs. C. I do not wish to hear.

Com. But I want to—

Mrs. C. I won't listen to you (*goes toward* D. L. 1).

Com. But you must.

Mrs. C. I won't. (*Exit* D. L. 1, *shuts and locks door.*)

Mer. (*coming from behind screen*) Has she gone. I'm glad you hid me, old fellow.

Com. (*dryly*) So am I.

Mer. She appeared slightly agitated; what have you been doing to worry her so?

Com. Nothing whatever; it is simply a woman's whim.

Mer. Ah! that accounts for it; I never could understand these women. But say, old man, don't you think you are a little hard on her, she seems very fond of you.

Com. (*indifferently*) You think so?

Mer. Yes, judging from appearances.

Com. That's just the trouble. I don't object to her being fond of me—in fact, I rather admire her taste—but I don't like her to show it. (*Aside*) Not to-day at least.

Mer. But don't you think you ought to make some allowance? Perhaps she is naturally of a suspicious nature, and possessing a deep feeling for you—as her benefactor you know—she is jealous when you show attention to others.

Com. But I am not attentive to others.

Mer. Perhaps not, Dickie, perhaps not; you used to be, you know.

Com. (*angrily*) Confound it! Merrigale, I know more about this matter than you.

Mer. Well you ought to.

Com. (*aside*) I wish I didn't. (*To* Mer.) And your advice is not asked or wanted.

Mer. Now, don't get angry, old man; no offense intended, I assure you.

Com. Well, please drop the subject, once and for all.

Mer. Certainly, if you wish it. (*Enter* Harris D. F.)

Har. The man wants to know, sir, how long he has to wait before you pay him, sir.

Com. What man?

Har. The man 'as brought them boxes, sir; he's waitin' ever since he came.

Com. Of course he has, you idiot.

Har. Yes, sir.

Com. I didn't ask him to wait.

HAR. Nor me neither, sir.

COM. Why didn't you tell me before? Send him up; but no, I will go down. (*Aside*) I don't want the fellow to blurt out anything about my wife, before Merrigale. (*Exit* COM. D. F.)

MER. Harris, where is Mrs. Meander?

HAR. I don't know, sir; fightin' with her husband, I reckon.

MER. Her what!

HAR. Her husband, sir; maybe you thinks as Mrs. Meander hadn't a husband, but she has.

MER. I don't understand this.

HAR. There ain't nothin' to understand.

MER. Who is her husband? Not Dick's—I—I mean Mr. Comfort's uncle!

HAR. Why, in course; she's his aunt.

MER. But why did she change her name?

HAR. (*chuckling*) I guess that's what he often wonders, sir.

MER. (*aside*) This is very singular; why does she take the name of Meander instead of Comfort. If I could only have a talk with that charming housekeeper, perhaps she could explain matters; there is certainly some mystery about Dick's relations.

MER. (*To* HAR.) I would like to have a few moments' conversation with the housekeeper.

HAR. (*surprised*) The housekeeper! We ain't got no housekeeper, sir; the house keeps itself, except when Mrs. Comfort keeps it.

MER. Mrs. Comfort! You don't mean the old lady?

HAR. That aint for me to say, sir, although I believe Mr. Comfort does call her that sometimes (*laughs*).

MER. But I didn't know she lived here.

HAR. Not live here! She's here most of the time, sir, except when she's away. She stays in town sometimes, sir.

MER. (*aside*) No wonder Dick is worried; I suppose these two women quarrel all the time. (*To* HAR.) Where is the maid? I wish to see her.

HAR. The maid, sir!

MER. (*sharply*) Yes, the house-maid; you seem surprised at everything I say; Sally, I think her name is; I thought she was the housekeeper. (*Aside*) These servants are always jealous of one another.

HAR. Sally ain't no more the housekeeper than I am, sir.

MER. Well, whether she is or not, I wish to see her; tell her to come here.

Har. Yes, sir. (*Aside*) What's he want with Sally I wonder. (*Exit* Harris D. L. 2.)

Mer. Very mysterious, very! (*Enter* Mean. D. R.) (*Aside*) Here comes old comfortable, evidently just awakened. (*To* Mean.) Well, sir, did you succeed?

Mean. (*sharply*) Succeed! Succeed in what?

Mer. In raising the roof; I left you hard at work. Your efforts certainly merited success.

Mean. Your words are meaningless. You left me very abruptly, interrupting my remarks in an extremely rude manner, sir.

Mer. (*laughing*) Ha-ha-ha, what are you talking about? It was you who interrupted my remarks. You snored so loudly that I had to stop my story—it was a good one, too.

Mean. Snore! I never snore, sir; never!

Mer. (*sarcastically*) Of course not; I suppose you never fall asleep either. You were not napping in the smoking-room, were you?

Mean. Certainly not, sir; certainly not. No doubt you were asleep yourself.

Mer. Yes, no doubt, and dreamed that I was you; what nonsense! All I have to say is, that if what I heard isn't a sample of your snoring powers, I don't care to hear one. (*Aside*) Thunder storms always frighten me. (*To* Mean.) No wonder you and your wife are always quarreling.

Mean. (*angrily*) How dare you make slighting remarks in reference to my family affairs! You know nothing about such matters.

Mer. No, I'm a bachelor.

Mean. That accounts for your ignorance; how true it is, " He jests at scars who never felt a wound." (*Musingly*) A bachelor! How sweet the word sounds. Young man, in order that you may learn never to jest about matrimonial affairs, I will tell you a story. (*Sits.*)

Mer. You wouldn't listen to mine.

Mean. Yours was told to provoke laughter and mirth, mine teaches a good and wholesome lesson.

Mer. (*aside*) Evidently nothing witty is to be expected (*sits*).

Mean. The story is a sad and doleful one; short, but full of pathos.

Mer. (*aside, taking out handkerchief*) The prospect is gloomy.

Mean. Long ago—(*musingly*) How long it seems.

Mer. How long ago did you say?

MEAN. I did not say. Long ago, a young man, then at the age of thirty-five.

MER. (*aside*) A mere child.

MEAN. Met an attractive young widow—

MER (*interrupting*) Fell in love, they were married and lived happily ever after; moral, always marry widows; those stories are all alike.

MEAN. (*with dignity*) You will be kind enough not to interrupt. It is true, the young man fell desperately in love.

MER. (*half aside*) Of course, they all do.

MEAN. His love was returned—

MER. C. O. D.?

MEAN. (*angrily*) Your jesting is exceedingly malapropos, sir. You will kindly allow me to finish my story in my own way.

MER. Certainly, sir, this is your story.

MEAN. You seem to have forgotten the fact. As I remarked, the young man's affection was reciprocated.

MER. (*aside*) The widow was evidently a Republican.

MEAN. They were married, but contrary to all expectations, they did not live happily.

MER (*aside*) An exceptional case.

MEAN. The wife did her utmost to provoke the husband's wrath.

MER. Of course the wife was to blame for everything.

MEAN. Certainly, sir! for everything!

MER. (*sarcastically*) They always are.

MEAN. Always. She had been so accustomed to managing her first husband—who was an invalid—that she expected " number two " to yield everything also.

MER. But " number two " thought differently.

MEAN. Yes, sir, very differently. *He* doesn't yield everything; oh no! far from it.

MER. That is certainly a tale of woe.

MEAN. (*impressively*) Young man, I stand before you the living example of what an unhappy married life will do. (*Slowly and solemnly*) I married that widow.

MER. Well, judging from appearances, I should *hardly* call you a happy man.

MEAN. Far from it, and yet I have my happy moments.

MER. Impossible!

MEAN. These quarrels with my wife are only occasional, and when the eagle of gory war has taken his flight and the white dove of peace once again hovers over our lives, then we are happy as of yore.

MER.   Well, if I were you, I would wring that gory eagle's neck and cage the dove of peace; then you could keep it by you.

MEAN.   Your metaphors are mixed.

MER.   Perhaps they are; I don't often dabble in metaphors. (*Enter* MRS. M. D. L. 2.)

MEAN.   Many times have I regretted that I ever married. I was a young fool then.

MRS. M.   Yes—you're older now. (MEAN *and* MER. *start.*)

MER. (*aside*) Now for a scene.   Perhaps I can prevent one.   (*To* MRS. M.) Madam, your husband was just speaking of you.

MRS. M. (*dryly*) Yes, I heard it.

MER.   But—a—madam, you misunderstand; I meant favorably of course, favorably.

MRS. M.   It sounded so.

MER.   He was saying how sad he felt that husband and wife were always quarreling.

MEAN.   I said nothing of the kind, Merriblow.

MER.   Well—of—a—of course not those words exactly, but—a—they—had that meaning, I'm sure they had.

MRS. M.   Young man, I am not in need of an interpreter, my hearing is still good, and I wish to say, that the name denoting foolishness, is, in my opinion, very appropriate to this—this person; if he had called himself an idiot, he would have spoken the truth also.

MEAN.   Merriblow, she is a good judge of idiots.

MRS. M.   I ought to be.

MEAN.   That's so, she ought to be.

MER.   My dear friends, this is terrible, do try to control yourselves.

MEAN.   I have no doubt I was an idiot when I married.

MRS. M.   And never got over it.

MEAN.   Ha-ha. I suppose you, I mean she, thinks that awfully funny.

MRS. M.   He seems to enjoy it. It is exceedingly appropriate for nobody to laugh at nothing.

MEAN.   She calls herself " nothing;" I was trying to laugh at her.

MRS. M.   He couldn't find a better subject.

MEAN.   No, not to laugh at. (*Enter* COMFORT D. F.)

MER.   My dear, sir, for the love of peace, do be calm; these remarks will only create trouble. (*Sees* COM.) Ah, Dick, do try and pacify your uncle and aunt, they have been—a—been misunderstanding each other.

Mrs. M. *You* were not asked to interfere, sir.

Mean. The matter does not concern you in the least.

Mer. Thank Heaven, there is one point upon which you agree.

Mer. (*aside to* Com.) Dick, can't you reconcile them?

Com. (*aside to* Mer.) Suppose you withdraw and I will try the part of peacemaker.

Mer. (*aside to* Com.) I wish you luck; I will go clothe myself in my own garments—they must be ready for me by this time—these are becoming a little too monotonous. (*Exit* Mer. D. L. 2.)

Com. Uncle Meander, wouldn't you like to go in the smoking-room and—

Mean. (*interrupting*) No, I wouldn't; I don't smoke, I told you, and I have spent far too much valuable time in that room for one day.

Com. Well, then, one of these other rooms (*pointing to the left*).

Mean. No, that is the enemy's country.

Mrs. M. Richard, there is no necessity for him to withdraw; I consider *my* time too valuable to waste here.

Com. My dear aunt, I do not wish to disturb you, I—

Mrs. M. It will be a pleasure to go; there are some unpleasant remembrances, Richard, which one is glad to leave behind. (*Exit* Mrs. M. D. L. 2, *haughtily*.)

Mean. That cut was meant for me. (*Laughs weakly*.)

Com. (*after pause*) Uncle, don't you think it a pity that you and Aunt Clementina quarrel so continually?

Mean. Yes, Richard, I am willing to confess I do think it a pity. But we do not quarrel continually, oh no! only occasionally. This happens to be a little stronger than usual, that's all. Still, I think it a pity, a great pity.

Com. Then why do you do it?

Mean. I don't; it isn't my fault.

Com. Oh! that's always the way!

Mean. Yes, always.

Com. Adam started the fashion by blaming Eve, and ever since then husbands have been unwilling to think themselves in the wrong.

Mean. Then it is Adam's fault.

Com. I've no doubt you are to blame just as much as Aunt Clementina.

Mean. Well, perhaps you are right. I do not enjoy being at enmity with my wife, but—a—

Com. But you do not know how to alter matters? I'll

tell you. Go to Aunt Clementina, tell her that you are sorry for what has happened and—

MEAN. (*interrupting*) Oh! I couldn't do that.

COM. It is the only way.

MEAN. Imagine my telling her I was sorry; the shock would kill her.

COM. Oh! no, not so bad as that, although no doubt it would be a surprise.

MEAN. I should say so.

`COM. A pleasant one, though. Come now, uncle, prove to her it is the unexpected that always happens; that there *is* something new under the sun.

MEAN. Richard, my boy, I believe you are right. (*Taking his hand*) I'll try it. You ought to be a married man; I believe you would make a good one.

COM. (*eagerly*) You think so.

MEAN. But, you're *not* married, and I guess it's just as well. (*Enter* SALLY D. F.)

SAL. I come as soon as I could lave my work, sor.

MEAN. (*angrily*) Who asked you to come at all! In my opinion the sooner you "lave" here the better.

SAL. I knows thim as doesn't ask ye're opinion. (*To* COM.) I was informed thet there circus clown was after wantin' to say me, sor.

MEAN. Well, he's "after wantin' to say" you now, so, Sally, you may leave the room.

SAL. Me name's not Sally, me name's "Sarie" in Frinch.

MEAN. I don't care what you're name is in "Frinch" or Chinese or any other language; it's Sally in English. (*Enter* MRS. M. D. L. 2.)

MRS. M. Sarah, go pack my bag instantly!

SAL. Why, mum, I thought—

MRS. M. No matter what you thought; instantly! do you hear!

SAL. Yes'm, I 'ears. (*Exit* D. L. 2.)

MEAN. My dear Clementina, I want to—

MRS. M. (*snappishly*) Hold your tongue, sir; how dare you call me by my maiden name!

MEAN. (*aside to* COM.) Now, whose fault was that?

COM. (*aside to* MEAN.) Don't you see she is in a temper?

MEAN. (*aside to* COM.) That's nothing unusual.

COM. (*aside to* MEAN.) You ought to speak to her when she can listen to reason.

MEAN. (*aside to* COM.) She never can.

COM. Not now, while she is excited. (*To* MRS. M.) My

dear aunt, why do you wish your bag packed? You are not going to leave, are you?

MRS. M. (*sarcastically*) Oh! certainly not, I expect to stay forever.

COM. (*aside*) I hope not. (*Aside to* MEAN.) Uncle, I think you had better retire, until the storm blows over; come with me into the garden. (*To* MRS. M.) Aunt Clementina, you will excuse us, while I show uncle the grounds?

MEAN. Just as you think best Richard, I shall go and get my hat. (*Exit* D. R.)

MRS. M. I think a little air would do your uncle much good.

COM. (*aside*) It is easy enough to play the part of a sign-post and point the way of peace to unhappy couples, but unfortunately the sign-post remains in the same spot. I wish some one would show *me* the way to peace with my wife. (*Enter* MEAN. D. R.) (*To* MEAN.) Are you ready, uncle. (*Exit* MEAN and COM. D. F.)

MRS. M. I can't endure it, and I sha'n't endure it. I shall not remain here to be insulted. He treats me shamefully, outrageously! Poor dear Mr. Barnes never treated me so. And then he blames me for everything when it is always his fault. If he would only acknowledge that he is in the wrong I could forgive him, but unless he does, we shall be strangers forever. (*Enter* MRS. C. D. L. I.)

MRS. C. (*not perceiving* MRS. M.) I *must* see him.

MRS. M. (*sharply*) See whom?

MRS. C. (*starting—aside*) That woman here!

MRS. M. (*aside*) Sarah should have packed my bag by this time. (*To* MRS. C.) Just run up to my room and tell my maid I wish to see her, will you?

MRS. C. (*haughtily*) I am not accustomed to receive commands from strangers.

MRS. M. (*sarcastically*) Oh! you are not? (*aside*) We'll see as to that. (*To* MRS. C.) What difference does it make whether I am a stranger to you or not? As long as I am in Mr. Comfort's house and—

MRS. C. What right have you to be here?

MRS. M. What right! You are impudence personified! I have every right! What business is it of yours?

MRS. C. (*quietly*) I think Mr. Comfort has made it my business.

MRS. M. Made it your business! it's false! go, do as I bid you immediately! do you hear!

MRS. C. And what right have you to give me orders?

MRS. M. Mr. Comfort has certainly given *me* a right. I

am a very dear relation of his; (*half aside*) I am sure his *dearest* relation.

MRS. C. It isn't true! you came here just to make trouble; you can't deny it! you are trying to win his affection from me; but you can't succeed, he loves me, and me alone.

MRS. M. Loves you! (*aside*) The girl must be crazy. (*To* MRS. C.) Come, I have heard enough; I shall report what you have said to Mr. Comfort. You are presumptuous beyond all words!

MRS. C. (*excitedly*) You shall not remain in this house another moment; go! go I say! Leave instantly! (*calling*) Harris!

MRS. M. Do you, a mere servant, a common maid, dare to address me in this manner! I shall report you immediately; we will see which one shall leave; you or I— we'll see. (*Exit* D. L. 2.)

MRS. C. That woman *shall* leave. (*calling*) Harris! (*Enter* HAR. D. F.)

HAR. Yes, sir, I—mean ma'am.

MRS. C. Where is Mr. Comfort?

HAR. In the garding, watchin' the rosebugs, as it were, ma'am.

MRS. C. Tell him I wish to see him right away.

HAR. He's showing the old gentleman around the ground, ma'am; pointin' out the beauties of the spot, as he said, ma'am, the perspective on one thing an' another, as it were.

MRS. C. Did you hear me! I desire to see him immediately.

HAR. Yes, sir, I—I mean ma'am. (*Aside*) I'm afeared we're goin to 'ave a squall. (*Exit* D. F.)

MRS. C. Dick must send her away, or I shall go. Can it be that he no longer loves me? That he cares for this other woman? I hate her! I never was so unhappy in all my life; but sooner than remain and see him make love to another, I will separate from him forever. I *will* if it kills! (*Throws herself into a chair and cries.*) (*Enter* SALLY D. L. 2 —bringing bag.*)

SALLY (*throwing bag on floor*) There's her auld packed bag. I'm jist wurked to dith, thet's what I am. (*seeing* MRS. C.) Yez lazy crature! settin' round a' doin' nothin'. Where's Mr. Comfort? (MRS. COMFORT *stops crying*.) What yez cryin' about; yez big blubberin' baby yez. Where's Mr. Comfort, I asked yez?

MRS. C. (*wiping her eyes*) How dare you speak to me so?

3

SALLY. How dare me! ha-ha—did yez iver hear the loike of that! how dare me! I dare spake to yez or iny other man loike yez, jist as I think bist, an the sooner yez know that, the bitter it'll be for yez.

MRS. C. (*rising*) Leave the room instantly!

SALLY. An' thet's jist what I'll do, but not from iny of yez tellin' me. I'm glad to git out of the soight of the loikes of yez. I'll tell on yez, niver be afeared of thet!

MRS. C. Leave, do you hear!

SALLY. The missus will know that yez wouldn't till a leddy where Mr. Comfort were; yez great big overdressed, blubberin' baby yez. Why don't yez driss loike a female maid thet yez be, an' not be a-puttin' on airs loike a leddy thet yez aren't. I'll tell on yez! (*Exit* D. L. 2.)

MRS. C. What *does* this mean?

SALLY (*without*) Git out of me way, yez circus clown yez. (*Enter* MER. D. L. 2, *dressed in own suit.*)

MER. (*looking off* D. L. 2) A very impudent maid! there is too much French about her, that's the trouble; now if she were only Irish she might not be so exuberant and—a— and hilarious. (*Seeing* MRS. COM. *confused*) I—I beg your pardon, madam, I—I should say miss; I beg your pardon; do I—do I intrude? I—I was looking for Dick—Mr. Comfort, you know. (*Aside*) What a refined looking girl.

MRS. C. I expect Mr. C. here presently; may I—may I ask your name?

MER. Certainly, ma'am, certainly. (*Aside*) Charming manners; Dick is a brute. (*A pause.*)

MRS. C. And pray what is your name?

MER. Merrigale, madam, I—I mean miss, Mr. George Merrigale.

MRS. C. Mr. Merrigale! why I have frequently heard Mr. Comfort speak of you; you are an old friend of his, are you not?

MER. I flatter myself to that extent.

MRS. C. (*hesitating*) Then as a friend, perhaps—perhaps you will tell me whether you have noticed anything peculiar in his actions to-day; do you think he has been working too hard?

MER. Yes, no doubt that is it; been working too hard of course; hard work will tell on the best of us, you know; I never could stand it. (*Aside*) I think Dick is going crazy myself, but it wouldn't do to tell her so.

MRS. C. He has been acting so strangely toward me, ever since early this morning; he has never been this way before. I was beginning to fear that he cared for—that it was some other—trouble, but it can't be that, oh no! it can't be that. It must be overwork.

MER. Of course; Dick always was a hard worker.

MRS. C. You—you never thought—I—I mean you never noticed that he—he cared for—I should say, was attentive to any woman, did you?

MER. Well no, not recently; but to speak the truth, Dick was once very much in love with—

MRS. C. In love! with whom?

MER. (*quickly*) Oh! that was sometime—a very *long* time ago. Some think he got over it, in fact, he himself told me only to-day that he cared for no woman, but I do not believe it. I know more about this matter than people imagine and I have overheard some things which make me certain that Dick loves her still.

MRS. C. (*excitedly*) It's false, sir! I do not believe a word of it; you know it is untrue!

MER. (*aside*) By jove! what an idiot I am to tell her this. (*To* MRS. C) No, of course not, certainly it isn't true. I've no doubt the whole story is entirely without foundation. (*Enter* MRS. M. D. L. 2.)

MRS. M. So you refused to tell my maid where Mr. Comfort was, did you? You shall pay for it! I shall seek him myself, and when I find him you shall leave the house. (*Exit* D. F.)

MRS. C. (*half aside*) That woman again! she maddens me! (*To* MER.) Tell me, who is she? do you know?

MER. Why, that's Mrs. Comfort!

MRS. C. Mrs. Comfort? you are deceiving me?

MER. No, I am sure of it.

MRS. C. It's not true! I am Mrs. Comfort.

MER. (*astonished*) You, Mrs. Comfort! I—I did not know you were married. (*Enter* COM., MRS. M. and MEAN. D. F.)

MRS. C. I repeat, sir, I am Richard Comfort's wife.

MER. Dick's wife!

MRS. M. What's this?

MRS. C. (*turning*) There stands my husband and having a legal right as his wife, I demand that that woman (*points to* MRS. M.) leave the house. *Tableau.*

Curtain.

ACT III.

SCENE.—*Same as Act I and II.*

(MER. *discovered front of stage reading paper.*) It's of no use. (*Lays paper down*) My thoughts will wander. I will make one more mighty effort to forget the past. (*Takes up paper upside-down and attempts to read*) I can't do it. I have lost all interest in the news of the day; even prize fights have no charm. What can it all mean?

Dick's wife! He declared he was unmarried. It seems to be only a question of which one is to be believed; the benefit of the doubt belongs to the lady. Perhaps he is ashamed of her, but why? I don't understand it. (*As if struck by a sudden thought*) By jove! I see it! Dick must have married his maid and naturally is ashamed to confess it, especially as his uncle seems averse to his marrying. He can't have been married very long, for it has only been about a year since he was engaged to—a—that other girl. What was her name? I have forgotten it. No doubt she heard of his attentions to this maid and broke the engagement. (*Enter* HAR. D. F.)

HAR. Did you see Sally, sir? I sent her to you.

MER. Yes, I saw her; where is Mrs. Comfort?

HAR. I don' know where she is just now, sir; with Mr. Comfort, I reckon; they has had a little squall, sir, as it were.

MER. I don't mean Mr. Comfort's aunt.

HAR. I didn't think as you did, sir; I didn't, nuther.

MER. (*aside*) Can it be that he doesn't know Dick is married; I must go cautiously. (*To* HAR.) I mean Sally; the maid, you know.

HAR. Yes, sir, I know Sally's the maid. You said Mrs. Comfort, sir. I reckon Mr. Comfort wouldn't like to have his wife called a maid; leastways I wouldn't.

MER. No, of course he wouldn't.

HAR. But you did it, sir; you asked me where Mrs. Comfort were and then said you meant Sally.

MER. (*aside*) He evidently suspects nothing; Dick is keeping it a close secret.

36

HAR. Mrs. Comfort doesn't look any more like Sally, sir, then I look like a ton of coal.

MER. Mrs. who?

HAR. Yes, sir.

MER. What did you say?

HAR. Like a ton of coal, sir.

MER. No, no; who was the person that was unlike Sally?

HAR. Mrs. Comfort, sir.

MER. You mean old Mrs. Comfort, of course.

HAR. She aint old, sir.

MER. Well, that's a matter of opinion.

HAR. She's young and pretty.

MER. Pretty! That's a matter of opinion also. (*Aside*) The idea of calling Dick's aunt young and pretty. (*To* HAR.) I can't say, Harris, that I admire your taste.

HAR. Why Mr. Comfort wouldn't never have married her, if he hadn't thought her pretty, sir, no more than I wouldn't.

MER. The old man drew a blank then, that is to say, as far as her looks are concerned.

HAR. The old man, sir!

MER. (*angrily*) Yes, the old man; are you deaf?

HAR. What do you mean, sir.

MER. What in the thunder do *you* mean? Why you're dumb, jackassly dumb!

HAR. Just as you say, sir, (*aside*) it strikes me he's the dumb one; what's he mean by "old Mr. Comfort?" (*To* MER.) I was talking about Mr. Richard, sir.

MER. No, you weren't; you said Mr. Comfort's wife didn't look like Sally.

HAR. Neither she do, sir.

MER. Great scott! man! do you know who his wife is?

HAR. In course I do; I've knowed who she is for nigh on a year.

MER. A year! Not a year!

HAR. Yes, sir, ever since they was engaged and long afore it was told to nobody, sir. I always did like Miss Edith.

MER. Edith! Edith who!

HAR. I said *Miss* Edith, sir; Miss Edith Barley in course; leastways that were her name afore she married Mr. Comfort.

MER. Edith Barley! that was the girl Dick was engaged to.

HAR. In course, sir—that's what I said.

MER.   But he is married—(*hesitates.*)

HAR.   Certainly, sir, I said that too.

MER. (*aside*)   That is terrible! evidently this fellow does not know the truth. (*To* HAR.) And where is Mrs. Comfort now?

HAR.   Don't know where she is just now, sir; reckon she's somewhere around.   She's almost always to home, except when she is in town at her mother's, sir, and she's there pretty regular every week, as it were.

MER. (*aside*)   I must see Dick, and receive an explanation. (*To* HAR.) Tell Mr. Comfort I wish to have an interview with him.

HAR.   Yes. sir. (*Aside*) He seems to like to interview folks. (*Exit* D. F.)

MER.   Two wives! I always thought Dick a little gay, but this is carrying gayety to an extreme; it is positively festive.   Terrible! disgraceful! and Dick swore he was unmarried too. (*Enter* MEAN. and MRS. M. D. L. 2.)

MEAN.   My dear Clementine, I agree with you in everything.

MER. (*aside*)   Another wonder! I will speak to him about Dick.

MEAN.   What you say is certainly true; Richard must explain matters.

MER.   Just what I was thinking, sir.

MEAN. (*seeing* MER.—*sharply*) And what right have you to think anything?

MER.   What right, sir! I think—

MEAN.   Entirely too much.

MRS. M.   Entirely!

MEAN.   You think it your duty to interfere in every one's business, and do your utmost to make trouble between my wife and me.

MER.   Oh! pardon me, sir, I tried to smooth matters—

MEAN.   Smooth your grannie! there was nothing to smooth.

MRS. M.   Certainly not! you cannot smooth the placid mirror-like waters of a limpid lake.

MEAN.   And a lot of wind only ruffles the surface.

MER.   Yes, of course, but I was trying to pour oil on the already ruffled waters.

MEAN.   Your attempt was a failure.

MER. (*half aside*) I am aware of that fact.

MEAN.   A rip-saw cannot smooth.

MER.   I never imagined it could, sir.

MRS. M. (*sharply*) Then don't try it.

MER.   Thanks, I won't.   (*Aside*) They seem in a strangely agreeable mood.   (*To* MEAN.)   My dear sir, there is a little matter—

MEAN.   I have no time for trifles.

MER.   If your wife would kindly withdraw I—

MEAN.   My wife withdraw! Never!

MRS. M.   Nothing shall ever part us.

MER. (*aside*) Then I won't attempt it. A very loving couple.   (*To* MEAN.)   I am extremely glad to see you such a happy family, but—

MEAN.   I have no secrets from my wife.

MRS. M. (*to* MER.) If it be necessary for some one to withdraw you may do so.   (*Sits* C.)

MEAN.   We give you our full permission.   (*Enter* COM. D. L. I.)

COM. (*aside*) She refuses to be reconciled.

MER.   Ah! Dick! I wish to speak to you about—about something.

MEAN.   Richard, I would like to have a few moments of your valuable time.

COM.   I seem to be in demand.

MER.   Dick, if you'll come into the smoking-room we—

MEAN.   You will remain here, sir!

MER.   But I sent for him and I think—

MEAN.   Your thoughts are worthless.

COM. (*aside*) I evidently have no choice in the matter.

MEAN.   As Richard's uncle, I certainly have a right to the first interview.

COM. (*aside*) I had better remain and do my best to weather the storm.   (*To* MER.)   Uncle is right, and as in all other things, I will try to please him in this.

MEAN.   It is well that you know your duty. Sit down!

COM.   I am not tired, sir.

MEAN.   Sit down, I say!   (*Sits* R. C.)

COM. (*aside*) The storm is going to be a heavy one. (*Sits* L. C. MER. *stands by left side of* MEAN. *chair.*)

MEAN.   Richard, I desire an explanation, I demand one!

COM.   In any way that I can be of assistance, sir—in what—

MEAN.   You need ask no questions, sir, leave that to me. My wife has been insulted.

MRS. M.   Insulted by a common house-maid.

COM.   Impossible!

MEAN. (*angrily*) What do you mean, sir! you know it is possible! very possible! I demand an explanation.

Com. (*aside*) It is to be a thunder storm. (*To* Mean.) Why, uncle, *I* didn't insult her.

Mean. You did, sir! or if you didn't you allowed it to be done, which is the same thing.

Mrs. M. Precisely! the maid is in your employ.

Com. Yes, she is in—

Mrs. M. She must get out.

Com. But, my dear Aunt—

Mrs. M. You refuse to dismiss her? (*Aside to* Mean.) There may be some truth in our suspicions.

Mean. Richard, there is another matter.

Com. (*aside*) The storm is about to burst.

Mean. You know my wishes in regard to marrying, or rather to your not marrying. What did that maid mean by calling herself your wife?

Com. I'm sure I can't say, sir.

Mer. Why, Dick, you know—

Mean. Who asked you to interrupt, sir? (*To* Com.) Richard, how can you account for what she said?

Com. I—I can't account for it; she must be weak-minded.

Mer. (*aside*) What a liar he is!

Mean. You say then that you are not married to that maid?

Com. I am married to *no* maid.

Mer. Dick, how can you stand there and—

Mean. Mind your own business, sir! (*Rises*) What affair is it of yours whether Richard is standing or sitting? What difference would it make to you if he were married to ten thousand maids?

Mrs. M. He has a right to marry whom he pleases—

Mean. Without consulting you?

Com. (*aside*) I came out of that storm with great credit; I had better withdraw before the wind blows from some unexpected quarter. (*Rises*) (*To* Mer.) What was it you wished to say to me, George?

Mer. If you don't mind, we will adjourn to the smoking room. I—I imagine your uncle and aunt do not appreciate my society.

Mrs. M. Remember, Richard, you must dismiss that maid.

Mean. Yes, I do not propose that my wife shall be insulted.

Com. (*aside*) Dismiss my own wife! What am I to do? (*Exeunt* Mer. and Com. d. r.)

Mrs. M. I cannot understand it. That woman distinctly

said that Richard was her husband. What object did she have in saying so?

MEAN. It *does* seem mysterious, my dear (*sits* R. C.); but Richard vows there is no truth in it—you heard him—and we certainly should believe our nephew before a common kitchen-maid. No doubt, as he says, the girl is weak-minded. Perhaps she wishes to marry him, and the wish being the father to the thought, she thinks herself married.

MRS. M. But if she be crazy, why does Richard retain her?

MEAN. Can't imagine, my dear; but she shall not remain; I will see to it. I sha'n't allow strangers to insult my wife.

MRS. M. But you would allow acquaintances?

MEAN. Certainly not, my dear.

MRS. M. And you will never quarrel with me again?

MEAN. Never again; but it takes two to make a quarrel, you know.

MRS. M. More often, *one.*

MEAN. Oh! no, one cannot quarrel without the other.

MRS. M. But *one* can start a quarrel.

MEAN. Yes, that is true; but the past is forgiven, I do not blame you, my dear.

MRS. M. Blame me! I should say not; you have nothing to blame.

MEAN. I simply referred to our quarrels, my dear.

MRS. M. I was never to blame.

MEAN. Oh! come now, Clementina, I have no doubt we were both—

MRS. M. Speak for yourself, sir.

MEAN. You fly into a temper so easily, that it is utterly useless to try to reason with you.

MRS. M. Yes, for *you* to attempt to reason; you can't do it.

MEAN. My dear Clementina, you must not—

MRS. M. Must not! I shall do as I please. (*Sarcastically*) I thought you would never quarrel with me again. Oh no! never again! The truth is, you have such a disagreeable disposition that you can't control yourself.

MEAN. (*Quietly*) Then my darling—

MRS. M. How dare you talk so coolly! (*rises*) you hypocrite! you know you are in a raging temper; yes you are, you needn't deny it; I see it in your eyes. (MEAN *tries to speak*) Not another word, sir! I won't listen to you. Not one word! (*Exit* MRS. M. D. L. 2.)

MEAN. Now was that a quarrel or not? I didn't quarrel. She said she saw temper in my eyes; what's the matter with my eyes! they are not crossed.   Sorry that this should have happened; very sorry. After such an amicable settlement of our last disagreement; but deuce take it, I'm not going to apologize and tell her that I was to blame for this, when I wasn't. (*Enter* MER. D. R.)

MER. (*speaking out* D. R.)   Well, Dick, it is none of my business—

COM. (*without*)   Then why do you make it yours?

MER. (*speaking out* D. R.)   But you really oughtn't to act this way and you know it.

COM. (*without*)   If I know it, why do you tell me?

MER. (*as if to himself*)   He is irreclaimable, incorrigible! I can do nothing with him.

MEAN.   That's not to be wondered at.

MER.   No, you are right; when a man becomes a bigamist or a polygamist he is generally beyond recall.

MEAN.   You are talking at random—mere nonsense.

MER.   I wish I were, for Dick's sake.

MEAN.   What has Richard to do with it?

MER.   Simply this; Dick denies that he is married.   I say it is not true!

MEAN.   Of course it is untrue.

MER.   I mean what he says is not true. Dick is not only married to his maid-servant, but he has another wife.

MEAN.   What! Two wives! Impossible! (*Rises.*)

MER.   Improbable you mean, but I fear very possible. That he has two wives I am certain; the question is, where has he drawn the line? Upon investigation the number may multiply.

MEAN.   I do not believe it, sir! Upon what grounds do you make such an accusation?

MER.   First, the maid herself—

MEAN.   A weak-minded creature.

MER.   You think so, perhaps, but judging from a conversation I overheard there is more truth in what she says than you imagine.

MEAN.   Nonsense! What did you hear?

MER.   Enough, when added to what Harris told me, to confirm my suspicions.

MEAN.   What was that?

MER.   Just as I have told you, that Dick has two wives.

MEAN.   I do not believe a word of it, but—a—(*sarcastically*) your knowledge is unlimited—who is the other one?

MER.   The girl Dick was engaged to a year ago.

MEAN.   How's that? The girl he was engaged to!

Now I am sure that your suspicions are unfounded; he said the engagement was broken.

MER. Yes, but—a—any one can lie.

MEAN. (*angrily*) Hang it! No doubt you can, but my nephew is no liar. What reason would he have for keeping his marriage a secret?

MER. None, unless he had one wife already, or, perhaps he thought you would not favor it.

MEAN. Nor would I; I often told him so. Can it be true! But I will soon learn the truth. (*Goes toward* D. R.) No, it would be better to have more substantial proofs than those you have given me before accusing him. Where is this maid? I will see her first.

MER. I shall send her to you, sir; you will learn that what I say is true. (*Exit* MER. D. F.)

MEAN. This is scandalous! simply scandalous! But it can't be true! there must be some mistake! two wives! poor fellow; what does he do when he quarrels with both of them at once, or—a—or rather when they quarrel with him? The storm must be terrible. (*Enter* MRS. C. D. L. I. *Aside*) Ah, here is the maid; not a bad looking girl. (*To* MRS. C.) My dear, I desire a few moments' conversation with you; (*aside*) it is best to speak to her kindly.

MRS. C. Is this Mr. Meander, Dick's uncle?

MEAN. Yes, I am Mr. Comfort's uncle.

MRS. C. Dick told me that you were here, but—

MEAN. Mr. Comfort, my dear! Mr. Comfort! You should not be so familiar.

MRS. C. I—I forgot; but you are not company, and I call him "Dick."

MEAN. But a maid has no right—

MRS. C. I am not a maid; I am Dick's wife. Why he told you that I was a maid I—I do not know, unless—unless he has another wife (*beginning to cry*).

MEAN. Now don't cry. (*Aside*) What shall I do with her? (*To* MRS. C.) Richard has no wife, I am sure of it (*quickly*) except you of course.

MRS. C. (*crying*) But he has; I—I know it.

MEAN. (*aside*) When a woman *knows* a thing it is useless to try to convince her to the contrary.

MRS. C. She is in the house. I saw him making love to her.

MEAN. What! you saw him! here! This is outrageous! Are you sure?

MRS. C. Certain.

MEAN. My dear young woman, have you any proof

that you are Richard's wife—the marriage papers, for instance?

MRS. C.   I have them in my room.

MEAN.   And you saw him making love to another woman? The villain!   You're sure it was a woman?

MRS. C.   Quite sure.

MEAN. (*aside*) My temper is rising rapidly to fever heat. What a terrible look my eyes must have in them.   And so Richard has deceived me, has he?   Sally, are you aware—

MRS. C.   My name is Edith, sir.

MEAN.   Edith! He told me it was Sally.   Another deception!   Edith, do you know how your husband makes his living; what business is he in?

MRS. C.   None, at present, sir; he—he told me that you made him an annual allowance; is that true?

MEAN.   Alas! too true!   But do you know the conditions of that allowance?

MRS. C.   No, sir.

MEAN.   That he should never marry.

MRS. C.   He did not tell me that.

MEAN.   Of course he didn't, the rascal!   Still another deception!   And this is the way that I am to be treated by my own nephew!   A nephew that I have loved!   I'll not stand it!   He's had his day; now I shall have mine.   He's had his laugh; it is my turn, and we'll see who will laugh the longest and best; we'll see!

MRS. C.   Oh, uncle! please don't be too severe with poor Dick; for I love him still, it is not his fault, I'm sure it isn't; it is that hateful, old woman; if he will only give her up—

MEAN.   And he shall give her up.   I will dismiss her myself; where is she?

MRS. C. (*throwing arms about him*) You are very kind, but please spare Dick.

MEAN. (*aside*) She's a dear little creature. (*To* MRS. C.) I cannot spare him. (*Enter* MRS. M. D. L. 2. *horrified.*)

MRS. C.   For my sake.

MEAN. (*aside*) What would my wife say, if she saw me now? (*To* MRS. C.) Well, for your sake, I will try—I say I will try—to be less severe; but I must speak to him.   I shall do so now; he is in the smoking-room. (*Goes toward* D. R.)

MRS. C.   It is not his fault; I am sure of it. (*Exit* MEAN. D. R.)

MRS. M. (*angrily*) But it's your fault, you—you—I don't know any term strong enough for you.   You are not content with disgracing Mr. Comfort's good name, by calling yourself his wife, but you must try by underhand means to win the affections of another woman's husband.

MRS. C. I—I do not understand you: how dare you insinuate such a thing!

MRS. M. I dare speak the truth.

MRS. C. You know *that* is untrue. Once again I command you to leave the house.

MRS. M. And I defy you. (*Sitting*) I shall sit down here and remain until I wish to go.

MRS. C. You refuse to leave?

MRS. M. Certainly; until some one who has authority tells me to go.

MRS. C. Since you will not obey me, I shall bring some one whose authority you will be compelled to recognize. (*Exit* D. R.)

MRS. M. She is certainly crazy. (*Enter* MRS. C. and MEAN. D. R.)

MEAN. (*aside to* MRS. C.) Where is she?

MRS. C. (*aside to* MEAN.) Sitting there; she refuses to leave.

MEAN. (*aside to* MRS. C.) She does, does she? She won't remain long. (*To* MRS. M. *not recognizing her*) You refuse to go at this lady's bidding? perhaps you will obey my command. Leave this house immediately and forever! and if you dare to—(MRS. M. *rises*) my wife!

MRS. M. (*very haughtily*) I shall obey you; I leave this house and you, now and for—ev—er. (*Exits* D. L. 2) (MEAN. *sinks dejectedly into a chair.*)

MEAN. My wife!

MRS. C. Your wife! Oh! what have I done!

MEAN. And what have I done!

MRS. C. I was told that she was Mrs. Comfort; Dick's wife.

MEAN. Oh! wretched man that I am! This is the grand climax; the final to all our quarrels; she is going away forever. (*Rising—vehemently*) She must not go! I will speak to her (*goes toward* D. L. 2) (*stopping.*) But she will not believe me; why should she? I wouldn't believe myself.

MRS. C. Oh, uncle! I am sorry—

MEAN. So am I, my dear, but it wasn't your fault; you were misinformed. I should have recognized my own wife. What is to be done! You must help me. Come, we will see her and try to explain matters.

MRS. C. But—a—

MEAN. (*leading her toward* D. L. 2) You must go with me,

my dear; she would not believe me; come! (*Enter* MER. D. F.)

MER.   Sally will be here—

MEAN.   Confound Sally! Get out of my way, sir. (*Exeunt* MEAN. and MRS. C. D. L. 2.)

MER.   He has evidently been having a talk with Sally, and from his actions rather a stormy one. (*Enter* COM. D. R.)

COM. (*not seeing* MEAN.) They worry me almost crazy talking nonsense.

MER.   I should think your conscience would worry you.

COM.   Why should it?

MER.   Perhaps you have none.

COM. (*coolly*) Merrigale, I believe you're—a—you're a fool.

MER. (*quietly*) Thank you.

COM.   You wished to speak to me—and then asked a lot of rubbish about my two wives; now what in the thunder do you mean? Is it a joke? It is a deuced poor one, and I fail to see the point.

MER.   But, Dick, you can't deny that you—

COM.   That I have two wives? I can and do deny it.

MER.   Oh! of course you *can.*

COM. (*angrily*) And I mean it too. I am becoming tired of your interference. Why did you tell my wife that I—

MER.   You confess then that you have a wife?

COM.   Certainly I do, but only one.

MER.   But you denied it at first.

COM.   For reasons which do not concern you in the slightest degree. I did not wish my uncle to know of my marriage; he was so averse to it. Now he knows everything, and a great deal more than everything, judging from the ridiculous way he has been talking about the crime of bigamy. What did you mean by telling Edith I had another wife?

MER.   Edith! I—I haven't seen her.

COM.   That's not true.

MER.   But it *is* true, Dick; I was talking to your other wife—I—I mean the maid.

COM.   Edith and the maid are one and the same; I called her that to deceive uncle.

MER.   What an idiot I am.

COM.   You certainly are.

MER.   And I told your uncle that you had two wives.

COM.   I wondered where he learned that rubbish; I thought it was not original with him. (*Sarcastically*) Merrigale, I am greatly indebted to you for all your trouble.

MER. But I—I really did not tell the maid—your wife I mean—that you had another wife.

COM. You pointed out some woman—I can't imagine whom—and called her " Mrs. Comfort."

MER. Yes, but I meant your aunt.

COM. My aunt! I have no aunt by that name. What! you didn't mean Aunt Clementina!

MER. The one that called herself " Mrs. Meander."

COM. *Called* herself " Mrs. Meander!" that is her name.

MER. Not her real name! I thought she was the wife of —is his name Meander? By Jove! I thought it was Comfort.

COM. Well, for a man of your years, you are the dumbest I have ever seen : a regular freak.

MER. You are right; dumb as a stone wall.

COM. I wish you were ; you would have said less.

MER. I am extremely sorry, old man—

COM. Oh! no doubt you are—but that doesn't help matters any. What is to be done? How am I to live? With the understanding that I should not marry, uncle made me a yearly allowance ; but no more help can be expected from that source.

MER. And it was through me that your uncle discovered the truth! What an unfriendly friend I am!

COM. You couldn't have done better—or rather worse— if you had been my enemy.

MER. Oh! don't say that, Dick ; don't make me feel any worse than I do already.

COM. Misery loves company ; you have succeeded in driving me almost crazy. (*Seeing papers on table*) Confound it ! here's my comedy, unfinished—I had forgotten it!

MER. Your what?

COM. My comedy ; I am writing a play.

MER. (*aside*) He has certainly gone crazy.

COM. It should have been completed by to-night; but it is too late now; it's too late! There have been so many interruptions—between the acts—that it will be impossible to finish it in time. A comedy! It should have been a tragedy ; then I could have played the star part.

MER. And it is all my fault! I feel so miserable that I would gladly take poison.

COM. Poison! would that this glass contained it (*takes up glass full of water, from table—Enter* SALLY D. F.) (*excitedly*) Poison! Death by it would be welcome! Then would I be at rest. Then would all these cares, worries, and false accusations be forever at an end. Poison! I would drink it as I do this—(SALLY *screams*—COM. *lets glass fall.*)

SALLY. He's pizaned! (*screams again*) Murder! Hilp! (*To* MER.) Why don' yez do somethin' an' not stand there loike a post thet yez are. Hilp! Where's the missus! I'll fitch her. (*Exit* SALLY D. L. 2.)

MER. She thinks you are poisoned. (COM. *stoops to pick up glass*) *Enter* MRS. C. *and* SALLY D. L. 2.)

SALLY. There he is, mum; all doubled up with spasms inside him.

MRS. C. (*running to* COM.) Oh, Dick! what have you done! Why did you do it. It is all my fault.

COM. But Edith I—

MRS. C. Do not attempt to speak; it will only weaken you. Sit down here (*pushing him into chair*) Quick! someone bring water!

COM. No, I object; no more water.

MRS. C. But you will die.

COM. Oh! no, I won't.

MRS. C. I implore you! do not die! live! live for my sake!

COM. Edith, I have no present intentions of dying; I feel better, much better (*attempts to rise*).

MRS. C. Do not rise! Not until you have entirely recovered. (*Kneeling*) Will you forgive me, Dick?

COM. Forgive you! What?

MRS. C. I have cruelly wronged you. I have entertained false suspicions; but I am so sorry, can you forgive me?

COM. Yes, what little I have to forgive. (*Enter* MEAN. *and* MRS. M. D. L. 2) But—a—but can you forgive me?

MRS. C. There is nothing—

COM. Everything, Edith! I have been a coward. I was afraid to tell uncle that you were my wife. Not because I was ashamed of you—I could never be that—but on account of uncle's wrath should he learn that I was married.

MRS. C. But it was for my sake.

COM. Yes, for your sake; but cowardly nevertheless. Oh! why didn't I tell you everything when we were married?

MRS. C. Never mind, dear; it is all over now.

COM. Yes, it is all over. I must seek some employment by which I can support you. Perhaps this play which I have been writing may bring me something. I cannot expect uncle to—

MEAN. (*stepping forward*) No, Richard, you can *expect*

nothing more from me. I blame you—not so much for marrying this dear little girl; she's a jewel; by Jove! if you hadn't married her, I would have done it myself.

MRS. M.   Sir!

MEAN.   Of course I—I mean if I had not met a very fine woman first, my love. (*To* COM.) But, Richard, I *do* blame you for not confiding everything in your wife.   As you say —you should *expect* nothing from me, but—here's my hand, young man (*giving hand*), I forgive you.

COM.   Sir!

MEAN.   For your wife's sake.

COM.   How can I thank you! I did not expect—

MEAN.   If you had, I wouldn't have done it.

MRS. M.   Your wife should be a blessing to you, Richard.

COM.   She has proven herself one.

MER.   Mrs. Meander, I think—

MEAN.   Let me advise you to stop thinking in future; it is a bad habit.   And now, Richard, a playwright's life is not a happy one; yours should be full of happiness.   Write plays for amusement, if you will, but when you are in need of the wherewithal to sustain life, draw on your uncle —Between the Acts.

Curtain.